P9-DCI-543

For Annie, Sophia, Laurie, Solomon,
and all the children of the city
K. H.

For my mum and dad
P. H.

Text copyright © 1996 by Kathy Henderson
Illustrations copyright © 1996 by Paul Howard
First U.S. edition 1996
Library of Congress Cataloging-in-Publication Data
Henderson, Kathy, date.
A year in the city / Kathy Henderson ; illustrated by Paul Howard. — 1st U.S. ed.
Summary: A month-by-month description in pictures and words of what goes on in a city during the year.
ISBN 1-56402-872-0
[1. City and town life — Fiction. 2. Seasons — Fiction.]
I. Howard, Paul, date, ill. II. Title.
PZ7.H8305Ye   1996
[E] — dc20   95-45095

2 4 6 8 10 9 7 5 3

This book was typeset in Stempel Schneidler.
The pictures were done in watercolor and crayon.
Printed in Hong Kong
Candlewick Press, 2067 Massachusetts Avenue,
Cambridge, Massachusetts 02140

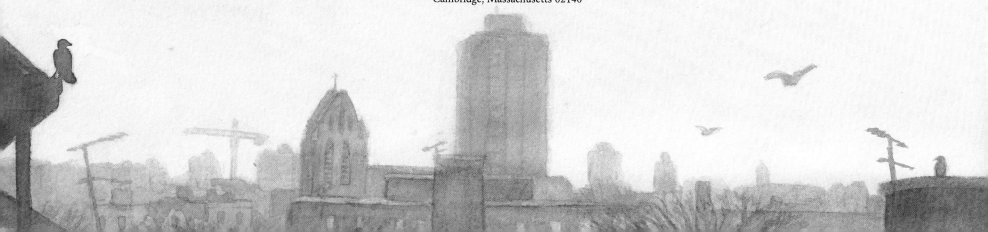

A YEAR IN THE CITY

Kathy Henderson

illustrated by Paul Howard

CANDLEWICK PRESS
CAMBRIDGE, MASSACHUSETTS

The year's turning, the year's turning

through the streets
and the houses
where the people pass
and the traffic churns,
all the time
the year keeps turning.

JANUARY starts.

It's dark in the morning
and the trees are as bare
as the TV antennas.
Everyone's leaving
to go to work.
There are the children
standing round the bus stop.
The drivers scrape ice
off their frozen cars.

Nobody talks.
They breathe out steam,
hurry along
past the cold street birds
and down the stairs
into the subway.

Rush.

Squash.

Squeeze.

Push.

Rattling warm
into the center
of town.

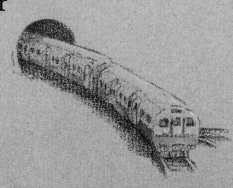

Hey look!
It's snowing!
Great flakes floating
out of the sky,
trying to turn the city white.
        Fat chance!
        Here come the children
        for a snowball fight.
The storekeepers grumble
and get out their shovels.
And the drivers?
        They just keep going.
        Wheels spin.
        Skid.
                Slide.

"Watch
    that car!"   CRASH!

FEBRUARY clatters.

Tin cans rattle.
A bitter wind lashes at the
trash in the gutter.
Sirens wail
and monsters roar.
Ooo-ee, ooo-ee.
There's a police car flashing by.
An ambulance races
close behind.

There's a helicopter
chattering in the sky
watching all the traffic.
Ooo-ee, ooo-ee.
And more:
there are the first snowdrops.
Through the crowds by the
restaurants in Chinatown
a paper lion leaps and sways
dancing the Chinese
New Year in.
The children laugh
and stare and cling.
And all the time
the cold wind sings.
Here comes spring.

MARCH stretches.

The days grow.
It's time to wash
the windows,
clean the house.

Look up there!
The tree men are cutting back
the sycamore trees
before the leaves come out.
They've got chainsaws roaring,
gnawing at the branches
till they fall into a tangle
on the road below.

And the street sweeper's out,
there's a truck cleaning drains,
the laundry lines are flapping
but here comes more rain.
A woman cleans windshields
when the traffic lights turn red
and even the buses at the station
take their turn
in the giant rollers
of the big bus wash.

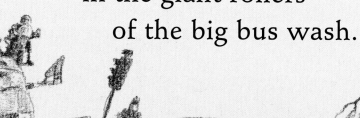

APRIL's bursting.

The supermarket's packed
with chocolate eggs
and fluffy chicks
and food for Passover,
and lines.
A workman slaps
a clean advertisement
over the torn one on the billboard.
"It's fresh!
It's new!
It's SPRING!"
it says.

At the petting zoo
by the railroad tracks
there are newborn piglets,
lambs, a calf.
And it's the Easter vacation,
there are children and babies
everywhere.

The sparrows up
in the broken gutter
line their nests
with candy wrappers.

Everything comes
out in MAY,
    trees,
      bike riders,
        and ice-cream signs.
      It's time to go
      to the park and play.
The daycare children
skip around throwing blossoms
at each other.
"Look at that jogger!"
"Funny shorts!"

"Can we feed the ducks?"
"Ooh, there's baby ones!"
At the restaurant
by the tennis courts
the old people talk,
    pigeons fight for crumbs.
      There's a wedding
      on the town hall steps.
      "Smile, please!"
      CLICK.
      "Thank you."

      Next thing
      you know,
      summer's here.

JUNE blooms.

The nights are short.
The air is full of grassy smells.
Very early in the morning
at the farmers' market
huge trucks drive in
from the countryside.

They're full of vegetables,
fruit, and flowers
picked from the fields
only hours ago.
Those yawning
storekeepers come to buy
produce for their stores
at opening time
and drive off through
the just-waking city.
Along the streets
the roses bloom,
hedges are clipped
and mowers drone,
and strange things grow
in the strangest places.

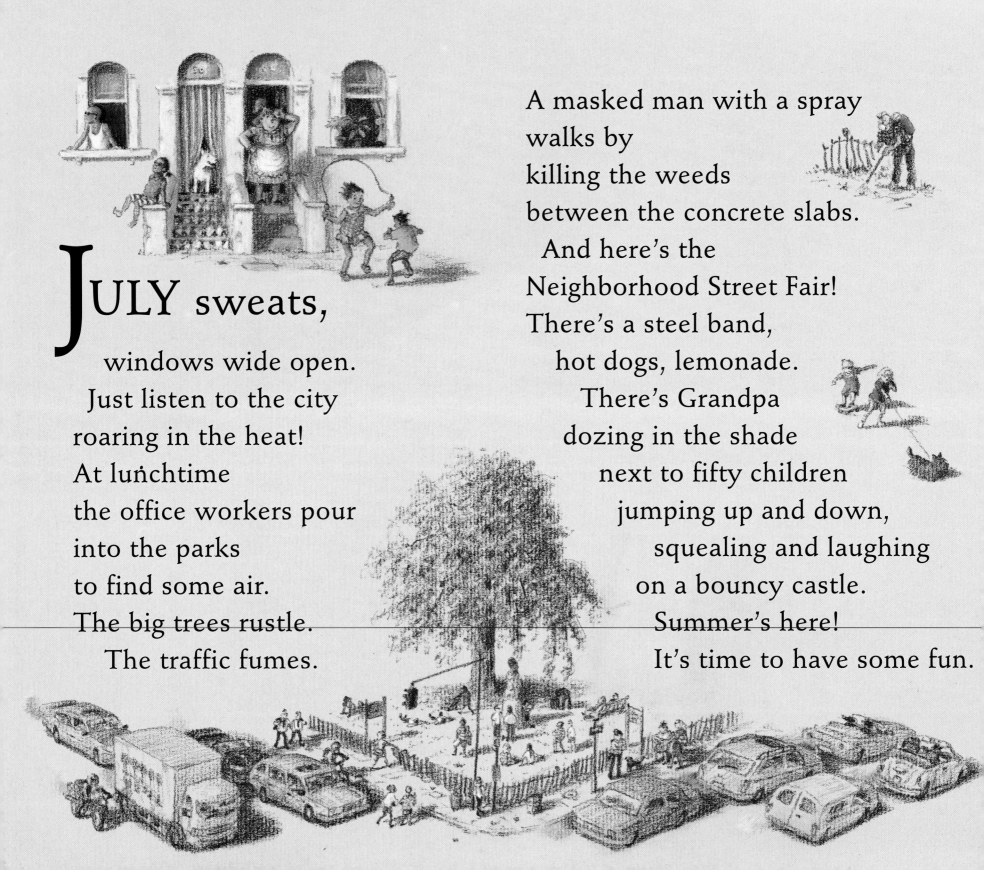

JULY sweats,
  windows wide open.
   Just listen to the city
roaring in the heat!
At lunchtime
the office workers pour
into the parks
to find some air.
The big trees rustle.
   The traffic fumes.

A masked man with a spray
walks by
killing the weeds
between the concrete slabs.
   And here's the
Neighborhood Street Fair!
There's a steel band,
   hot dogs, lemonade.
      There's Grandpa
dozing in the shade
      next to fifty children
      jumping up and down,
         squealing and laughing
      on a bouncy castle.
      Summer's here!
      It's time to have some fun.

Then
AUGUST sighs.

Trainloads of people
leave the stations.
Cars piled high
with tents, suitcases,
bathing suits, and suntan lotion
are setting off for the highways,
getting away for those easy days,
leaving the streets
to their August ways . . .

and to the tourists
who come in tall, cool buses
with their cameras and sunglasses.
They go for boat trips
on the river,
troop in and out
of museums and churches
and into the squares
to stand and stare
at dozy dogs on dusty doorsteps,
tired winds swirling the litter,
children flopping
in the sprinklers
trying to get cool.

August days are lazy days
and even the traffic's
half asleep.

Autumn's here!
SEPTEMBER snaps.
The roads hum.
Wake up! Time for work!
Children are going
back to school
with heavy bags
and stiff
new shoes.

The little ones
are clinging
to their parents' hands
all terror and excitement
on their first day
at school.

On Saturday
down at the soccer field
the season starts
and the big game brings
a crowd that sways
and chants and sings,
while out in the park
the first
leaves
fall.

OCTOBER pauses.

Golden. Still.
But there's so much work
to be done before winter.
There's the painter
hurrying to finish
the drainpipes
and the windowsills.
The roofers bang the last nails in
and take down
their scaffolding poles.

The children squabble for chestnuts.
Ice-cream trucks play hopeful tunes
but the candy store man
cleans his freezer,
"No more now
till next summer comes."
And down at the city gardens
there are potatoes and carrots
to dig up and store.

The days are shrinking,
the nights are growing,
and children dressed up
as witches and ghosts
haunt the sidewalks
calling, "Trick or treat?"

Then overnight
NOVEMBER strikes.

Now a cold wind
whips the branches,
strips the last leaves off the trees,
and chases them along the streets.
They block the drains.
Then it rains.
Big puddles grow
and passing traffic
throws up waves
of water at the forest of
umbrellas walking by.

At the doctors' office
the waiting room's full
of sniffing and coughing,
aching heads, and babies crying.
"Next please."

The doctors see them
one by one
but there are always
more to come
and the dark days get
still darker.

Winter's back.

Then the
lights
are lit.
DECEMBER glitters.
Shoppers crowd the sidewalks
by the big city stores
searching for gifts.
    See the Christmas trees?
    Where the warm air comes up
        from the subway

there's a woman on the
ground wrapped in
old coats and string.
She's got holes in her shoes.
She's got nowhere to sleep.
The carol singers
shake tin cans and sing
    and the crowds hustle by
    in their fancy clothes
        on their way to a show,
        going out, hurrying home.
            They'll be cozy inside
            while the dark days pass.
The stores close.
The holiday comes at last.

And when it's all over
and the table's cleared,
late on the last
night of December,
the wide-awake city
waits to hear
the clock
strike
midnight   because. . .
                The year's turning,
                the year's turning.
                See the people dance
                and kiss and sing?
                Hear the bells ring
                and the cars honk?
                Here's January again.
The years keep turning.